The lintel above my door reads 1656, a plague year, the year of my construction. I was built of stone and wood, but with the passage of time, my windows came to see, my eaves to hear. I saw families grow and trees fall. I heard laughter and guns. I came to know storms, hammers and saws, and, finally, desertion. Then, one day, children ventured beneath my shadow seeking mushrooms and chestnuts, and I was given new life at the dawn of a modern age. This is my story, from my old hill, of the twentieth century.   — The House, 2009

the House

ROBERTO INNOCENTI

J. PATRICK LEWIS

CREATIVE EDITIONS

Mankato

1900

I listen as the gossip-wind exhales,

Behold! The House of twenty thousand tales.

No longer shut away, a doomed outcast:

The children have discovered me at last.

1901

Each season watched my wilderness abide

The plague-and-ash-heap history of the hill,

Let time and toil temper me until

I feel my ancient stones refortified.

1905

The century but five years young takes root

In every infant grapevine and new shoot.

The founders of this little dynasty

Tend endlessly the hardy family tree.

1915

Midsummer's dress is maid-of-honor green.

The hill girl takes her future by the hand—

A mason-soldier from the bottomland.

Life holds its breath when weddings intervene.

1916

By spring's pastoral play, the hill, beguiled,

Returns a natural likeness: mother and child

Accepting Easter blessings. *Here, be peace.*

(May altar boys be spared two angry geese!)

1918

From wife to widow … and the depths of grief.

My furnace burns as children leave for school,

Bundled in virtue, books, and classroom fuel.

How beautiful their innocence, how brief.

1929

Empurpled is my speck of empire now:

The gift of grapes has won the cat's meow.

Cloud bottoms and the figure eights of flies:

What do such things foretell as west winds rise?

1936

Today begins a seasonal event:

We wage the timeless "battle of the wheat"

To scythe and winnow, knowing that defeat

Will harrow hope and harvest discontent.

1942

Catastrophe, despair and hatred chase

Victims far from the flames that light my face.

I am the final refuge of the poor,

Who suffer but in suffering endure.

1944

Whose war is this that lasts a thousand suns?

Relief born of fatigue describes the mood

Of partisan and peasant gratitude

For valor and a respite from the guns.

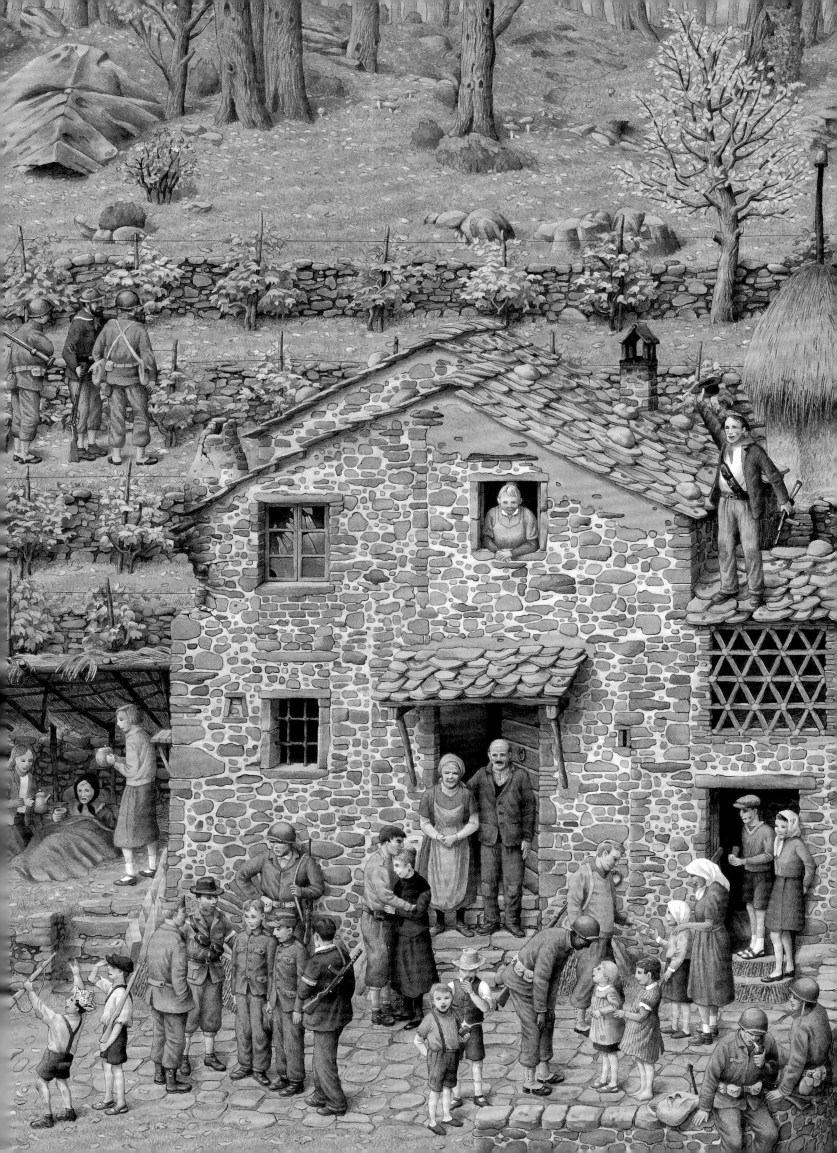

1958

The widow pours her milk and with a spoon

Stirs melancholy past the afternoon.

What bags her son has packed to move away

Contain all vestiges of yesterday.

1967

Now gather me a rainfall of farewell:

The widow's passing is my funeral hour.

A House without a heart is like a flower

Without the dew. And quietly tolls the bell.

1973

This generation has much youth to spare,

Yet old stones youth alone cannot repair.

I am a House but I am home to none;

My voyage to destiny is nearly done.

1993

Mold is my master after twenty years

And I am captive to this solitude.

Wild creatures and the elements intrude.

My cobblestone-work downs and disappears.

1999

A murmur on the breath of nightingales—

Where is the House of twenty thousand tales?

I do not recognize my new address.

What became of the maxim, More is less?

Yet always I shall feel the sun and rain,

True keepers of the deed to my domain.

Published in 2009 by Creative Editions

P.O. Box 227, Mankato, MN 56002 USA

Creative Editions is an imprint of The Creative Company.

Edited by Aaron Frisch. Designed by Rita Marshall.

Printed in Italy

Library of Congress Cataloging-in-Publication Data

Lewis, J. Patrick. The House / by J. Patrick Lewis;

illustrated by Roberto Innocenti.

ISBN 978-1-56846-201-

1. Children's poetry, American. 2. Dwellings—Juvenile poetry.

I. Innocenti, Roberto, ill. II. Title.

PS3562.E9465H68 2009   811'.54—dc22   2008040810

First Edition

2 4 6 8 9 7 5 3 1